THE Bravest Woman
IN AMERICA

BY Marissa Moss
ILLUSTRATIONS BY Andrea U'Ren

TRICYCLE PRESS
Berkeley

To Elias, the bravest, most determined person I know.
—M.M.

For these amazing two who sacrificed so much: my husband,
H-C Münchmeyer, and my amazing son, Sebastian. And for a
most wonderful editor, Joanne Chan Taylor.
—A.U.

Text copyright © 2011 by Marissa Moss
Illustrations copyright © 2011 by Andrea U'Ren

All rights reserved. Published in the United States
by Tricycle Press, an imprint of Random House Children's
Books, a division of Random House, Inc., New York.
www.randomhouse.com/kids

Tricycle Press and the Tricycle Press colophon are
registered trademarks of Random House, Inc.

Picture credit: Photograph of Ida Lewis courtesy
of Susan White Pieroth.

Library of Congress Cataloging-in-Publication Data
Moss, Marissa.
  The bravest woman in America : the story of Ida Lewis / by
Marissa Moss ; illustrated by Andrea U'Ren. — 1st ed.
    p. cm.
1. Lewis, Ida, 1842-1911. 2. Lighthouse keepers—Rhode
Island—Newport—Biography—Juvenile literature. 3.
Newport (R.I.)—Biography—Juvenile literature. I. Title.
  VK1140.L48M67 2011
  387.1'55092—dc22
  [B]
                2010008917

ISBN 978-1-58246-369-8 (hardcover)
ISBN 978-1-58246-400-8 (Gibraltar lib. bdg.)
Printed in China

Design by Katy Brown
Typeset in Caxton and Victorian
The illustrations in this book were rendered in watercolor,
ink, and acrylic on paper.

2 3 4 5 6—16 15 14 13 12 11

First Edition

Ida loved the sea. She loved it when it was calm and coppery in the sunlight.

She loved it when it was wild with froth, like a herd of stampeding horses. She loved the crash of the waves, the screech of gulls wheeling overhead, the bite of salt in her nose as she breathed in the ocean air.

She loved it all.

The oars were heavy and awkward, but Ida was stubborn. She pushed and pulled until the boat lurched forward. It was slow. It was hard. Her shoulders ached and her hands blistered.

But when the front of the boat bumped up against the small beach of Lime Rock, Ida felt a bubble of triumph lift her up. She'd made it!

From that day on, Ida rowed with Pa as often as she could. He told her stories about storms and drowning sailors, sinking boats and rescues.

He taught her how to check on the light—how to fill it with oil, trim the wick, and clean the lens.

Most of all, he taught her to row.

Over the years, Ida grew strong and lean. Now when she gripped the oars, the boat glided smoothly through the water. If the wind was wild, she knew how to lean into it. If the waves were high, she knew how to stay calm and let the sea break over her.

The oars were part of her now, and her strokes were sure and steady.

When Ida turned fifteen, she got the best birthday present she could have hoped for. The Lighthouse Board had decided that Lime Rock needed a keeper to live there at all times. There had been too many shipwrecks, too many lost boats. A full-time keeper would make the harbor safer.

So a house was built with a tower holding the light. It was a real, official lighthouse, and Ida and her family would be the first to live there.

Ida loved watching the sea for any sign of trouble. She loved polishing the lighthouse lens so the light would shine bright. She loved rowing her two younger brothers and her sister to school and back home every day.

"You're a real lighthouse keeper now," her sister told her.

"I think you're the bravest girl in America!" her youngest brother said.

"And you're definitely the best rower ever!" her other brother boasted.

Ida shook her head. "No, not yet. But someday I will be."

That day came sooner than Ida wanted. Pa got sick. He grew weaker and weaker every day until he was no longer able to care for the lighthouse. While Pa sat at the window watching the sea, a blanket wrapped around him, Ida and her mother kept the light full and strong, beaming over the water.

Ida was ready for the job. Like her father, she kept watch over the harbor, scanning the waves for any ship in trouble.

Ida had never seen her father rescue anyone, but he had told her how to haul people over the stern so they didn't tip her boat. He had described how to lift a man out of the water, how to warm him in blankets afterward so the chill didn't kill him. Ida felt ready for anything.

One winter evening, Ida spotted a small boat bobbing wildly in the harbor, tipping back and forth as a boy shinnied up the mast. The sun was setting, and Ida's first thought was that the boy was trying to get a better view of where to head. Then she heard laughter carried on the wind. Three other boys on the boat waved their arms at each other, whooping loudly. It was just a game, a bit of fun, but to Ida it looked dangerous.

She watched as the boat pitched over, throwing all four boys into the sea. Then she didn't watch anymore— she ran to her own small boat and rowed out to the boys.

It was darker now, the waves wilder, but she could hear yelling, and through the mist she could make out the upturned keel of the boat. The boys tried to cling to its slippery sides, but there was nothing to grip. Their legs churned the water in panic, their clothes weighed them down in the slapping waves, and the icy cold of the water made them gasp for breath.

Ida reached the first boy and grabbed him, just as her father had told her to. She pulled him into the boat, then quickly rowed around to reach the next boy, who was thrashing and spitting water. She hauled him in too, and then the next one, and then the next.

The boys' faces were white with cold, their lips blue. One passed out, lying limp on the bottom of the boat.

Ida didn't think. She rowed—harder and faster than she ever had. The waves crashed over her head, tilting the boat along a wall of green and gray. Ida kept on rowing, frantic to get them all to safety.

"I can do it," she told herself. "I have to do it."

When she pulled the boat onto the beach at Lime Rock, she threw down the oars and looked up, exhausted, into her mother's proud face. "Well done, Ida. Let's get these boys into the house," said Mrs. Lewis.

"They need to get warm and dried."

Once the boys had recovered and the seas
had calmed, Ida rowed them back to town.

Then she set her boat back toward the lighthouse. Each stroke of her oars brought her closer to her home, closer to where she belonged. When she got there, her father was waiting for her.

He didn't say anything, just hugged her hard.
Then he handed her his captain's hat. Ida was in
charge of the lighthouse now . . .

And she knew it.

Author's Note

IDA LEWIS, LIGHT-HOUSE KEEPER, NEWPORT, R. I.

Ida Lewis, born February 25, 1842, went on to rescue many more people after that first time when she was sixteen. She was sixty-three when she made her last rescue. Officially, she saved eighteen lives, but the real number may be as high as twenty-five. After her father's death, Ida's mother was made official keeper while Ida did the actual work. When her mother also died, Ida finally got the title to go with her lifelong work. For thirty-nine years, she was the keeper of Lime Rock. She was also known as "the Bravest Woman in America,"* and by Act of Congress in 1874 was recognized for her heroism with the Congressional Life Saving Medal. In 1907, a year after the American Cross of Honor was created by Act of Congress, Ida became the first woman to receive the award.

At a time when women couldn't vote and someone like Susan B. Anthony could ask "Are women persons?" Ida proved that a woman could be as brave as a man. "Anyone who thinks it is un-feminine to save lives has the brains of a donkey," she said in an interview. Thousands came to visit her each year, including President Ulysses S. Grant, General William Tecumseh Sherman, General Ambrose Burnside, and Admiral George Dewey.

Ida lived with her eye on the guiding beam of the lighthouse and the sea around it until her death in 1911 at the age of sixty-nine.

* According to *Harper's Weekly*, *New York Tribune*, and *Putnam's Magazine*